Santa Claus

Whispers

Written
by
Cher Louise
Jones

Illustrated
by
Lee Dixon

Feisty Kids Publications

Feisty Kids
is an imprint of

Feisty Scholar Publications

www.feistyscholar.com

Santa Claus Whispers

First Edition

978-1-913619-07-7 (paperback)

For news and details of upcoming publications from this author visit:

www.cherjones.co.uk

Whispers of Santa Claus carried on the breeze, to where icebergs float and teardrops freeze.

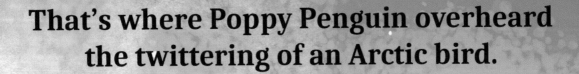

That's where Poppy Penguin overheard
the twittering of an Arctic bird.

"Santa Claus travels far and wide,
delivering presents to every child."

"But he doesn't do it by himself.
He has a team of trusty elves."

Then Poppy Penguin began to dream
of joining Santa's elven team.
"But how do I find the elves' workshop,
when I'm at the bottom of the world,
and Santa lives at the top?"

The Arctic terns had overheard
each of Poppy's whispered words.
"Silly penguin, you'll fly of course.
Just like us and Santa Claus!"

"Santa's the greatest pilot to ever fly.
He surfs the clouds across the sky.
He races comets and he swerves past stars.
He loops the loop his sleigh round Mars."

Poppy flapped her little wings...

but flying just was not her thing.

"We could carry you part way there."
Then they lifted Poppy into the air.

When the terns set Poppy down,
she was greeted by a roaring sound.
"Excuse me, my friend,
but have you seen
Santa and his reindeer team?"

"Of course!
He can weight-lift
elephants without a care,
and juggle hippos
high in the air!

Santa can lift the roof from off a house,
then he sneaks in quiet as a mouse.
Just like me, he's strong and brave.
And he'll leave a toy if you behave!"

Then Poppy told the lion of her dream
to become an elf on Santa's team.
"I'll have my kingdom lend a paw."

Then he told the animals with a roar
to help Poppy Penguin with her goal
to reach Santa up at the North Pole.

So Poppy was passed from hoof...

to tusk...

to hump...

to paw...

to wing...

to snout...

to horn...

to claw.

And as Poppy travelled across the land,
she heard rumours of this mighty man.
Poppy travelled day and night,
until the ocean was in sight.

From the water burst a massive tail
belonging to a beluga whale.
"Excuse me, my friend,
but have you seen
Santa and his reindeer team?"

"Of course!
Like me, he travels far and wide,
with Rudolph acting as his guide.

"He visits cloud castles
high up in the air.
Then climbs towering mountains
to deliver up there.

"He dives under the waves,
deep into the sea,
down to Atlantis,
where mermaids swim free.

"Farewell, my friend. I must leave you here."
And with a splash, he disappeared.
So Poppy wandered in the snow,
without a clue which way to go.

Then, from the dark and starry night
walked a man with a beard of white.
"I heard someone crying,"
the kind man said,
as he shivered in pyjamas striped with red.

"Why are you out here all alone,
so far from your South Pole home?"

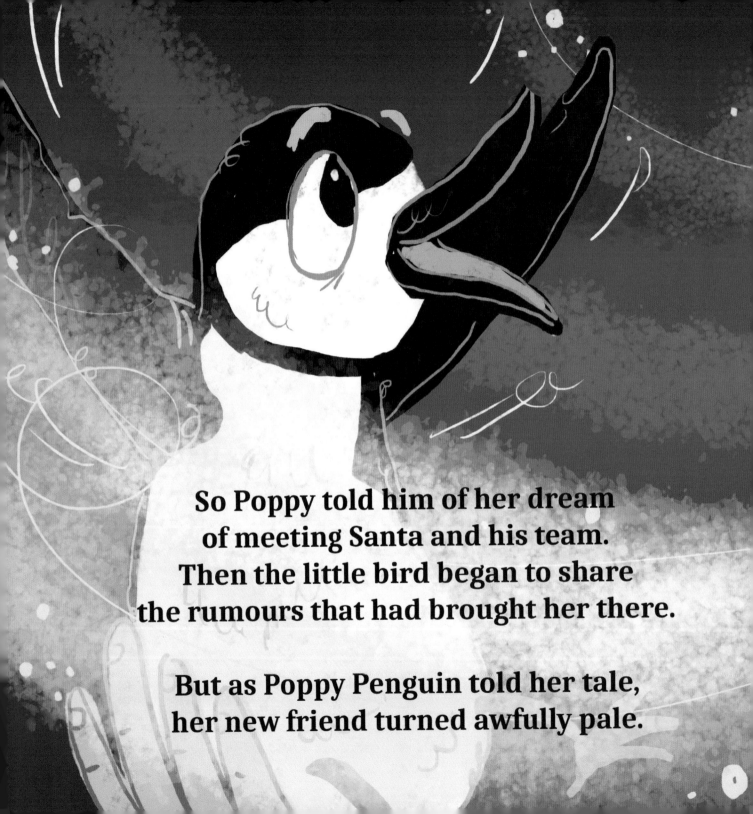

So Poppy told him of her dream
of meeting Santa and his team.
Then the little bird began to share
the rumours that had brought her there.

But as Poppy Penguin told her tale,
her new friend turned awfully pale.

"Come with me, and I'll let you know
something I learned years ago.
Sharing whispers are how rumours spread,
and they're often untrue," the wise man said.

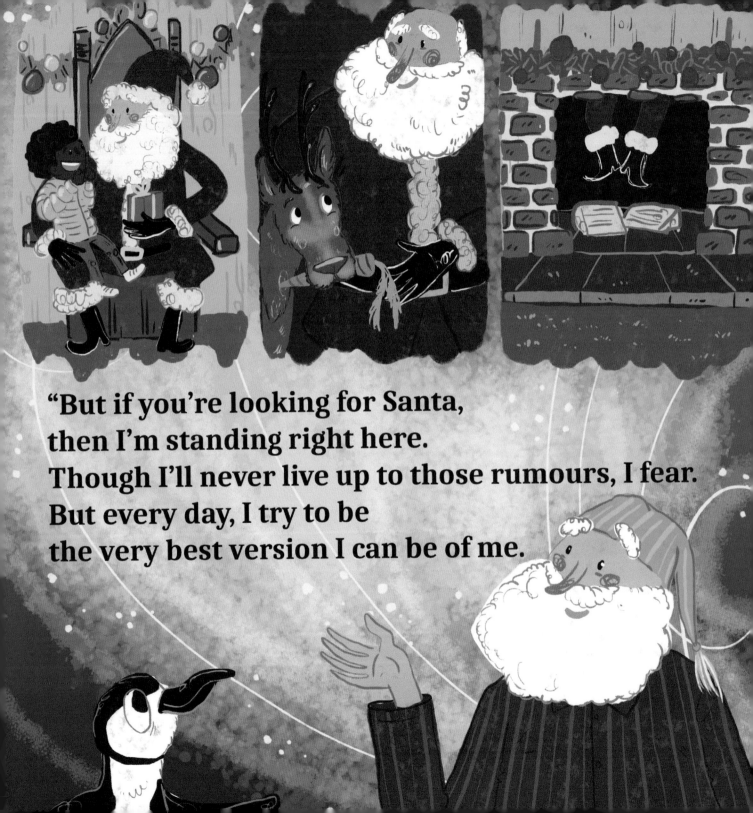

"But if you're looking for Santa,
then I'm standing right here.
Though I'll never live up to those rumours, I fear.
But every day, I try to be
the very best version I can be of me.

"Besides, you seem such a brave penguin yourself.
Have you ever considered becoming an elf?"

Other books available by
Cher Louise Jones:

Bigger Dreams

Walk Tall

Printed in Great Britain
by Amazon